JAY WILLIAMS

Puppy Pie

illustrated by

WAYNE BLICKENSTAFF

A MODERN MASTERS BOOK FOR CHILDREN
THE CROWELL-COLLIER PRESS

First Crowell-Collier Press Edition 1962

Library of Congress Catalog Card Number: 62-21355
Copyright ©1962 by The Crowell-Collier Publishing Company

Jenny was a little girl
who liked good things to eat.

She liked meat and potatoes
and ice cream.

She liked cake and turkey and fruit.
But most of all she loved . . .

APPLE PIE.

"It means that it is nice.

It means that it is sweet.

It means that it is good," said Jenny.

"It means that it is—*twingilly!*"

At Thanksgiving, Mother said,
"Shall I bake a pumpkin pie?"
"No, no," said Jenny. "Apple."

When Christmas came, Mother said,
"What shall we hang on the tree?"
Jenny said, "Apple pie!"

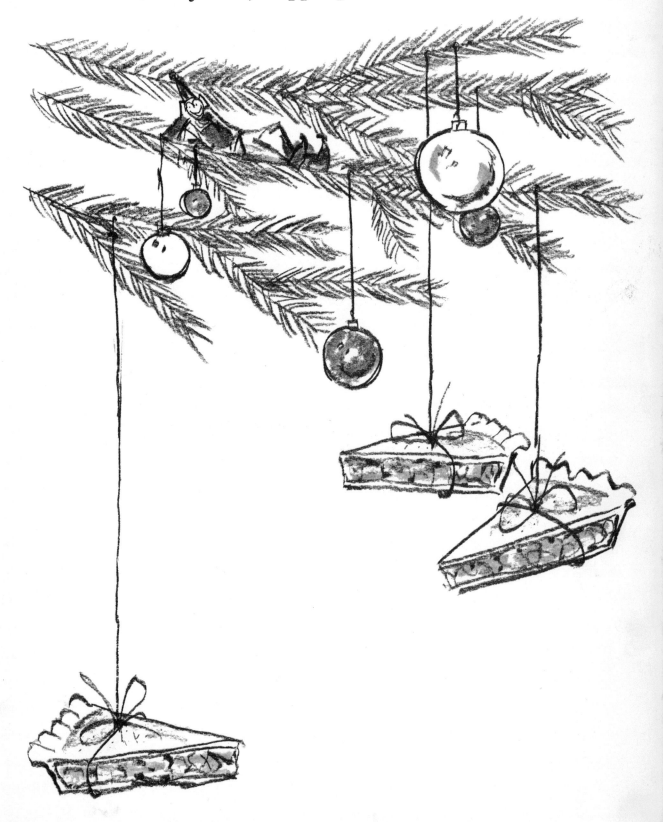

At Easter, Mother said,
"Shall we hunt for Easter Eggs?"
"I think Easter Pie would be better,"
said Jenny. "And make it out of apples."

Jenny loved apple pie today
and apple pie tomorrow.
She even loved apple pie yesterday.

When Mother asked why she loved apple pie
so much, Jenny made up a word for it.

She said, "I like it
because it is

TWINGILLY!"

"What does that mean?" asked Mother.

Jenny had a puppy.

He was a Christmas present.

His name was Sam.

Jenny was five years old.

Sam was five months old.

Jenny said, "We are the same age."

Jenny loved Sam more than she loved
apple pie. She played games with Sam.
She took Sam for walks. Sometimes
she played that she was a mother and
that Sam was a little boy. She would ask,
"What do you want for dinner, my little boy?"
Her little boy always wanted . . .

APPLE PIE.

Then Jenny would sing a song she had made up:

"Apple pie, apple pie,
I know I love it—
I don't know why.
I think it is *twingilly*,
Apple pie!"

ELLEN   ROBIN

When Jenny's birthday came, Mother said,
"We will have a party.
You may ask all your friends to come."
"Good!" said Jenny. "I will ask Ellen
and Robin and Debby. And I will ask
my best friend, Vicky."

DEBBY   VICKY

"Can we play some games?"

"Yes," said Mother. "And we will have
a birthday dinner. I must bake a good cake
for you, too. What kind shall it be?"

Jenny said, "Apple pie cake."

Mother laughed.

"I never heard of apple pie cake," she said.

"I am not sure I know how to bake one."

"Oh, it is not hard," said Jenny. "Just bake
an apple pie and we will put some candles on it."
"Very well," said Mother. "We will have
the party. We will have the dinner.
And you shall have your birthday pie."

Jenny
called
her
friends
on
the
telephone
and
asked
them
to
come
to
her
party.
They
all
said
they
would.

Mother cleaned the house
and Jenny helped her.

They set the table.
They made everything look pretty.

Then Mother said, "I think
I will bake the pie now."
She started to work.
"Please let me watch," said Jenny.

She called her puppy. She sat down
with one arm around Sam
and they both watched.

Mother got the pie all ready.

She made lots of dough and rolled it out.

She put some dough in a pan.

She cut up the apples. She put them on
the dough. She rolled out some more dough
and put it on the top for the crust.

There was some dough left over.

"What will you do with that?" Jenny asked.

Mother said, "I will bake it, too.

It will be a crust with no pie under it.

We can eat it like a big cookie."

She put the pie in the stove. She put the crust
with no pie under it in the stove, too.
"Soon they will be ready," she said.

Then she sang:
    "Apple pie, apple pie,
    I know I love it—
    I don't know why.
    I think it is *twingilly*,
    Apple pie!"

She skipped
into the garden with Sam.
"Oh, Sam," she said,
"What fun birthdays are!"

Then she sang:
> "Apple pie, apple pie,
> I know I love it —
> I don't know why.
> I think it is *twingilly*,
> Apple pie!"

She put the pie in the stove. She put the crust
with no pie under it in the stove, too.
"Soon they will be ready," she said.

The pie began to bake.
A sweet smell was in the kitchen.
"Oh," said Jenny, "It smells
TWINGILLY!"

"Sam," she said, "do you like birthdays?"

"Bow-wow!" said Sam.

"I know. That means *yes*," said Jenny.

"When is your birthday, Sam?"

"Bow-wow-wow!" said Sam.

"Today?" Jenny asked.

"Today is your birthday?
Yes, I see.
We are the same age.
When I was five,
you were five.
Now I am six,
so you are six, too."
"Bow-wow!" said Sam.

Jenny jumped up. "It is not fair if Sam
has nothing for his birthday," she said.
"I know. I will make a birthday pie
for him, just like mine."

She ran back to the house
and went into the kitchen.
Mother was not there.

Jenny got some dog food and put it
into a pan. She put some bread in it.
Then some fish from yesterday's dinner.
Then a little milk.

"There!" she said. "These are the things
a dog loves. This will be a fine surprise
for you, Sam. But I need something
to put on top. I need a top crust
so it will look like a real pie."

Jenny looked around. The apple birthday pie
had been baked. Mother had put it on the table
to cool. The crust with no pie under it
was baked, too, and Mother had put that
on the table next to the apple pie. Jenny
saw the round crust with no pie under it.
"This will be just right for Sam's pie," she said.

She took the round crust and put it
on top of the dog food, the bread,
the fish, and the milk.
Now Sam's pie looked like a real pie.
It looked just like the apple birthday pie.

Jenny said, "It looks *twingilly*, Sam.

It looks as *twingilly* as apple pie."

Then she made up some new words for her song.

She sang:
> "Birthday pie, birthday pie,
> I know I love it—
> I don't know why.
> Now Sam has a *twingilly*
> Birthday pie."

Jenny said, "Now I will let it cool
like a real pie."
She put it on the table next to the apple pie.
Then she ran to find her mother.

"Mother!" she said.

"Do you know what day this is?"

Mother laughed.

"Yes. It is your birthday, dear," she said.

"But it is Sam's birthday, too," said Jenny.

"Oh," said Mother. "How do you know?"

"He told me," said Jenny.

"And I baked a birthday pie for him.

Now I am going to find him a present."

She looked in her toy box.
She had all kinds of toys.
"Would Sam like a doll?" she said. "No,
I don't think so. Would he like a toy bunny?
Or would he like a blackboard?
Oh, dear, I do not think he would like
any of those things."

But at last she found a red rubber ball
in the toy box.
"Oh," she said, "I think
this is what Sam would like."
She got some pretty red paper.
She put the paper around the ball.
The present for Sam was ready.

First they played some games.

There were little presents for everybody.

There were lots of balloons.

There was lots of candy for everybody to take home.

Then Mother said it was time for dinner.

They were just about to sit down to dinner,

when Jenny jumped up.

They came at dinner time.

There were four girls who were Jenny's friends.

They were Ellen, Robin, Debby, and Vicky.

They were all wearing their best dresses.

They all said, "Happy Birthday, Jenny."

They gave her presents. And she showed them

the presents Mother and Daddy gave her—

a coloring set, some books,

and best of all, a new bicycle.

First they played some games.

There were little presents for everybody.

There were lots of balloons.

There was lots of candy for everybody to take home.

Then Mother said it was time for dinner.

They were just about to sit down to dinner,

when Jenny jumped up.

But at last she found a red rubber ball
in the toy box.
"Oh," she said, "I think
this is what Sam would like."
She got some pretty red paper.
She put the paper around the ball.
The present for Sam was ready.

It was almost time for the party. Everything was ready. Jenny put on her new blue dress. She put on her new party shoes. She waited for her friends to come.

"Oh!" she said. "I almost forgot Sam's present."

She got the ball and gave it to Sam.
Sam pulled the paper off with his teeth,
and ran after the ball.
"I think he is happy with that present,"
said Jenny's best friend, Vicky.
"I think he likes it."
"What else are you going to give him?" asked Robin.
Jenny said, "I have a surprise for him.
You will see."

She went into the kitchen. There were
the two pies on the table, side by side.
Jenny took one of them and put it on the floor.
That was for Sam.
She got a box of birthday candles and
put six candles on the crust of the other pie.
That was for her.
Then she went back to the party.

Daddy was home and he helped Mother.
They gave the children dinner.
There was chicken, ice cream, and cookies.
They ate and ate.

Then Mother said, "Now it is time
for the birthday pie." She put it on the table.
The candles gave a yellow light.
It looked very pretty.
Everybody sang the birthday song.

Daddy said, "Is everybody ready for some pie?"
He cut the pie.

Then a funny look came over his face.
"This does not smell like apple pie," he said.
From the pie came a smell of dog food,
bread, fish, and milk.
"My, my," said Daddy. "This does not look
like apple pie. It is a new kind of pie."

Mother looked
at the pie.
She laughed.
"It is puppy pie," she said.

Jenny ran to the kitchen. Her friends went with her.
Sam was not eating his pie. He smelled it.
He looked at Jenny. "Bow-wow-wow!" he said.
"What is he saying?" asked Ellen.

Jenny said, "He says
he does not like
apple pie.
He wants
puppy pie."

She gave Sam his own pie.
He was happy. He ate it.

Daddy took the apple pie back to the table.
"That was a birthday surprise for Sam,"
he said. "And it was a birthday surprise
for us, too! But now we shall have
the real birthday pie."
He cut the apple pie, and they all had some.

Jenny made up some new words for her song.

She sang:

    "Puppy pie, puppy pie,

    I love my Sam

    And he loves his pie.

    There is nothing nicer

    Than *twingilly* pie."

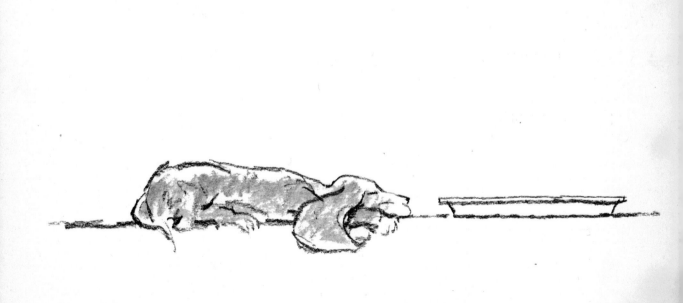

MODERN MASTERS BOOKS FOR CHILDREN

PHYLLIS McGINLEY
> The B Book (Illustrated by Robert Jones)

ROBERT GRAVES
> The Big Green Book (Illustrated by Maurice Sendak)

LOUIS UNTERMEYER
> One and One and One (Illustrated by Robert Jones)

JAY WILLIAMS
> Puppy Pie (Illustrated by Wayne Blickenstaff)

WILLIAM JAY SMITH
> What Did I See? (Illustrated by Don Almquist)

JOHN CIARDI
> The Wish Tree (Illustrated by Louis S. Glanzman)

SHIRLEY JACKSON
> Nine Magic Wishes (Illustrated by Lorraine Fox)

PAUL ENGLE
> Who's Afraid? (Illustrated by Ray Prohaska)

EVE MERRIAM
> Funny Town (Illustrated by Evaline Ness)

ARTHUR MILLER
> Jane's Blanket (Illustrated by Al Parker)